The Sea at Sunrise

Teague de La Plaine

www.teaguedelaplaine.com

Contents

Chapter One

THIS IS HOW I see the sea at sunrise: from my bed through a wall of glass, an impossible admixture of black water cut sharply with a horizontal line of blood-red smashing up against mottled orange-yellow-mango-tangerine that fades into the palest blue and back to midnight and black again, this time dotted with pinpricks of light.

Did I have a good night? Did I have a good life? Do I deserve to greet this particular day? Will this be the day that I have a shot at redemption? Will I get my photo opportunity?

They're just questions, aren't they? And so is this: will they come to visit me today?

I agonize over this like a spoiled princess deciding which shoes to put on. Like my daughter used to do when she was small.

"What shoes go with irritatingly cute?" she asked once.

"I'm going to be one of those things if you don't hurry up and get in the car: we're going to be late for school!" I said back to her.

"Can I take the purse Granny gave me?"

"No! Now put on your shoes and let's go, young lady!"

Tears.

Crap. Why was I always so impatient? Always so quick to judge, to try and control, to make the world and all the actors in it bend to *my* storyline?

And why now, of any possible time of my life, am I full of so many questions?

I wish they'd just show up already.

But, no. It's Saturday and the sun's just coming up and it's early and the kids are still sleeping and, Jesus, now I'm weeping again.

"Good morning, Jo!" The perpetually joyous Maude comes in with the tray of crappy breakfast: powdered eggs, turkey bacon, two slices of Wonder Bread toast with two little squares of butter wrapped in foil (which won't be enough butter, because I *like* butter), orange juice in a plastic cup with foil glued down on the top that I can never seem to peel open correctly, a styrofoam cup of lukewarm coffee, and identically-sized potato cubes.

Breakfast of champions, I muse.

"Breakfast of champions!" Maude sings.

I sigh and try for another glimpse of the sunrise. Something about the sun coming up fills me with hope. That maybe this will all work out for the good. That maybe the sun won't stop rising for me one day.

But the sunrise is gone. It's just a morning now. The shimmering orange circle comes up fast after it breaks the horizon. It's weird how the morning light starts way early—especially here on the coast where nautical twilight seems to last for hours—and then fades in less than a minute once the sun peeks its bloodshot eye over the edge of the world.

Maude pulls the shades against my protest and the glorious sunrise morning glow fades behind a gaudy seashell print on polyester floor-to-ceiling curtains.

I suddenly feel seasick.

My hands shake as I try and peel the foil off of the orange juice. The foil comes off in a rough strip, leaving the rest of itself stuck to the lip of the cup. But the hole is big enough and I gulp down two big sips, sticky 100% Florida gold running down one side of my chin.

Maude wipes it clean.

"How was your sleep?" she asks. "Any dreams worth remembering?"

"Nothing but nightmares, Maude," I sigh.

"Well, we deal with our stuff when we dream," she says.

She's right. Because being awake is more or less the same as nightmares. With fewer monsters but a lower chance of survival.

The diagnosis hit me pretty hard. Eddie just sat there, staring into the middle distance, saying nothing. It was the same face he made whenever he heard that one of his navy buddies had died in a car accident, or from cancer, or just from the body giving up after a hard life in the military.

I thought, *This is the worst thing that could happen.*

The doctor said, "This isn't the worst thing that could happen. The prognosis is pretty good."

But looking at Ed's face I knew the prognosis was crap: Eddie had already given up.

I spent the better part of the next year—our last year together, it would turn out—trying to convince him to fight harder, to stick around. But he had seen too much death, too many fights lost to cancer. He knew in his heart that it was a losing battle. He wasn't going to make it.

And that's how I feel now. And to hell with you, Eddie, for making me feel like this, like giving up. Because it's not the case that everyone dies from cancer.

"Nope," he would have said. "Folks die from lots of other things too."

In the end, he came around. He started fighting. He didn't want to leave me or our family or this world or this life. But it was too late. Somehow he thought that it didn't matter when you started fighting back. But it does. The *when* matters. You can't sit on it, ruminate, wait it out. You have to get on the offensive straight away. You have to tackle it. Otherwise, it tackles you.

"You just keep fighting, Jo," Maude says. She smiles and pats me on the shoulder and I want to smack her in the face.

"You have no idea what this is like," I say, looking her straight in the eye. But as soon as I say it, I know it's a lie. She may never have had cancer, but she deals with sick old meanies like me every day.

Suddenly, I cannot imagine what she must go through. Certainly, she bonds with her patients—even disagreeable ones like I can be sometimes. She has already learned so much about my life, about me. Surely she has bonded with me in her own nurse-like way. As she must have done with so many others. How old is she? What, forty? That's at least twenty years of working with people riddled with cancer, angrily trying to go to the bathroom on their own, vomiting from the treatment, sobbing and lamenting over lost hair, lost weight, lost friends, lost family, lost time. A lost battle for life.

How hard must *that* be for her to bear?

I struggle and manage to put a fairly convincing smile on my own face.

She smiles again, more softly. "It's going to be okay," she says. Then she leaves me with the rest of my crappy breakfast and the closed curtains and the antiseptic room.

I munch absently at the food. Could I keep fighting? *Should I?* It's hard to think of reasons anymore. Two, maybe: my daughter and *her* daughter. But they don't live close. And Ed's gone. My work is long past. All I really have is the sun rising over the sea each day. And how long will that keep me going? Sustain me?

One more day, at least.

Because the truth is that I *want* to see the sunrise tomorrow. I *need* to see the sunrise tomorrow. Seeing the sun rise has come to define my life, has created the fulcrum event that drives me forward, builds enough momentum that I can surf down the front edge of the sunshine just long enough to reach the night and surrender to the "false death" so that I don't slip into the real one.

The promise of tomorrow's sunshine puts me in the frame of mind to be purposeful with my day. Lying here with my tablet and stylus pencil making notes for my epic autobiography (which I will likely never publish—or even *finish*, let's be honest), the promise of tomorrow's sunshine reminds me to get to work as a human being. When I have trouble getting out of bed, I remember that I cannot complain about doing what I was made for, what I was meant to do in the world with this one, short little life I have been given. I was made to teach, to inspire the next generation. I spent my career teaching, and now that I have all the free time I yearned for in my working life, I can write everything down for the next set of growing humans to come along and discover. What's the alternative? As tempting as it would be to huddle under the blankets and stay warm and pretend I'm not dying, I have work to do.

How do I capture everything I've ever learned or experienced in a pithy sentence? Or even in a cumbersome memoir? It isn't possible, really. I've read plenty of memoirs—all of them by famous people. They have incredible stories. My life pales in comparison. And they also have ghostwriters who know how to tie words together and make them beautiful. And the actual discipline to finish something started. What do I have? A middle-class life. A boring—if honest—marriage. A love of sunrises. But what have I really done that makes it worth remembering? Even for me?

Maude interrupts my thoughts. Or maybe she expands on them. Coming through the door backward I can barely see what she's hunched over. It's a meal cart—but I already have my breakfast. She's being sneaky. But why?

She looks over her shoulder as she pulls the thing in, one bastard wheel squealing and flopping around. It makes my head hurt right behind my eyes and I squeeze them shut and when the sound stops and I open them again Maude has thrown open the shades and the mid-morning sun comes streaming in and glowing golden over the cart.

On top of the cart is a white cloth, draping over the sides and hiding most of the plastic structure. On top of the cloth are these: a dozen orange roses in a pale blue milk glass vase; a large white envelope with "Mrs. Kerner" written neatly on it; an unwrapped box of La Rochelle chocolates with a smart red bow attached to one corner; and a small square wrapped in sunrise orange paper, my favorite color.

Who would send these things? Who knew my favorite color of the sunrise? There are only two people who would send me any kind of gift at this point—and one of them's dead.

Maude rolls the cart close enough for me to reach it, but I hesitate, folding my hands in my lap. Maude takes away the breakfast things I didn't eat (most of it) and puts it on another cart out in the hallway. When she comes back, she sees I haven't moved. I can't stop staring at the envelope with my name on it. Whose handwriting is it? Who do I even know who cares to send me something? Or that I'm even here? And why "Mrs. Kerner?" Is this a holdover joke from Eddie? Some surprise time capsule he left with his lawyer friend, Ernesto?

"What do you want to see first?" Maude asks. She doesn't ask if I want help. She can see I am suddenly incapable of raising my arms. I open my mouth, but no sound comes out. "You can clearly see the flowers and the candy," she says. "The only mysteries are the envelope and the present."

"All the things are presents," I say, being difficult for no reason. "*That*," I say, nodding toward the little box, "is a wrapped gift."

Taking that as a cue, Maude picks up the small box (about the size of a deck of cards) and holds it out to me.

"Let's leave the *who* until the end," she says.

I lift my hands, heavy with anticipation and trepidation: that handwriting *could* be Eddie's. *Stop it! Eddie's gone kiddo.* I pull at the corners and the paper rips and comes spooling slipping off the gift and suddenly I'm holding a small midnight blue jewelry box and I lift the lid with terribly shaking hands and there, amidst the puffy white polyester stuffing, is a fine chain of gold. I gently pluck it up with my thumb and index finger and bring it out of the box. And there, dangling in front of me is the finest tiny orange seashell I have ever seen. The jeweler has worked a fragile lip of gold around the edges and into a loop where the chain passes through. The sun sparkles against the gold.

I'm speechless.

Maude gently takes the necklace from me and helps me tip my head forward while she fastens the clasp behind my neck. She twists the shell and lays it on my chest. The chain is long enough that I can see the shell when I look down. It's beautiful.

As I stare and touch the tiny marvel, Maude busies herself with putting the flowers on the table by my bed and opening the chocolates, and setting them within reach. I thought I would not be able to eat such things once I came here, but it turns out that the idea is this: whatever makes you happy, you should do it because this might be the last happiness you'll ever get to experience.

She passes the foot of the bed and squeezes my left foot, casting a warm smile at me before she leaves again. Looking over at the roses, I notice Maude has placed the card on the bed, resting up against the safety rail. I'm terrified to open it.

I go back to playing with my new seashell necklace. I look out at the sunny day, the sparkling waters, the waves frothing at the shore.

Later, I think. *I'll open it later.*

You may not be here later, says the mean voice in my head. It's Missy Blackburn's voice, her nasally third grade mewling full of negativity that I hear in my brain every time I try to think positively. I hated her then and I hate her now. So what if she was ten and one of my third-grade students? The thought suddenly makes me smile and I'm snapped back to the present moment.

And that is enough. This moment, this view, this necklace, these flowers. Ah, and let me just grab one of those chocolates.

Perfect.

Chapter Two

T HE SUN HASN'T RISEN yet, but it will soon.

Someone has left the sliding glass window ajar and I can hear the ocean, waves crashing against and grinding the sand out there in the darkness.

Sometimes I think this is the perfect moment, the pre-dawn. I know some sailor friends who love the sunset, who spend their lives watching for the "green flash" which I think is a myth. But it's this pre-dawn that is the marrow of existence. It's the moment before everything begins. It's the entire universe compressed into a single atom before the Big Bang. It's divine expectation. It's all the potential energy in each of us.

I'm holding the card in my hands. I want to wait for the sun to rise before I open it and read it. This morning I had the most irrational dream that Ed was pacing my room, angry and impatient with me for not opening it.

"I didn't send you the goddamn card, Jo!" he belted. "Just open it, for chrissakes!"

So I opened it and a cloud of black and green snakes came pouring out and over me and the bed and began to worm their way into my chest and belly where the cancer lives and I woke up screaming and sweating and the night nurse—Mackie—was there and after a little while everything was okay.

I've just been lying here since then, waiting for the sun to come up. And it's funny: once you've been awake this long you start to think maybe the sun *won't* come up today. Maybe that was it. Maybe yesterday was the last sunrise you were going to see and now it's all HEAVEN'S TO BETSY! WELCOME TO PERPETUAL NIGHT!

But the twilight gave up the game eventually. Then I knew the sun would be along shortly. And here it is.

We all have this idea that we're going to be *somebody*. But the problem is that even if I ended up being more of a somebody than somebody else, I was still less a somebody than other somebodies. It's about degrees. It's about a range. And most of us fall somewhere pretty strongly in the low middle. And that's okay.

Because nobody will remember you two generations from now. Unless you really are a somebody. Unless you cure cancer. Or bring all the nations or religions or some other disparate groups together. But even Nobel Prize winners aren't that lucky—I can't even name one.

Except maybe Barack Obama. And I'm not a hundred percent convinced he *deserved* his.

Anyway, I never knew my great-grandmother, for example. And she never knew me. Sure, I heard plenty of stories growing up. But those stories could have been about anyone. I didn't have any real connection to that person, even though we shared some DNA. And what would it have been like to know her? My grandmother was a sweet old lady, but by the time I was fifteen, she started forgetting who I was. She started forgetting a lot of things—and remembering a lot of things that never even happened. So what kind of existence is that? To be old and senile? What's the point of being alive if you aren't aware of everything you've lived?

Thank goodness I got to know my Abigail. And perhaps I should be thankful that my body will likely be gone before my mind is.

I'll never meet any of *her* children.

We're all just two generations away from obscurity, aren't we?

My hands have stopped trembling. My left hand toys with the gold-and-orange seashell necklace. My right hand holds the card, still closed. I steady my nerves and leave the necklace alone. I open the card.

The heavy paper stock is also orange and on the front is a tiny sailboat sailing away into a sunrise. I open it carefully, as though I might spill the boat and the sea and the sunrise onto the sheets if I am not gentle.

"Dear Mrs. Kerner," it begins. I let out a sobbing sigh; it's not from Ed. The relief is overwhelming. Although it shouldn't be a surprise and I should feel pretty ridiculous that I even thought it in the first place. But that's the funny thing about the heart: it wants what it wants, and to hell with reason. My heart *wanted* it to be from Ed. Wanted it to be from a *living* Ed, who would come strolling casually through the door and into the room, pushing my awful hospital lunch on a cart.

"Lez horz dervz," he would say in his horrid faux-French accent. "Lez Madams will be having zeh lambz a la bamz?" Oh, *god*, how my heart aches suddenly. I would even have been happy with a card from a *dead* Eddie, caught up in the post office quagmire for a dozen years or shipped delayed through a mail forwarder. *Anything.* Just a glimpse of my old Ed again.

I take a moment and let the faucets turn off slowly. I dry my cheeks on my vomit green hospital gown. How I hate this place at this moment. I just want to be home again.

The card is not from Rachel either. I'm always "Mama" in her letters.

It is a force of will to keep from glancing at the bottom to see who signed it. Eventually, I place my left hand over the bottom half of the card and slowly lower it as I read:

Dear Mrs. Kerner,

Decades ago, in a time that seems now like a dream, I met a woman. It was like an electric shock to my soul and this meeting sparked a dormant Thing that lay deep within me. This Thing is sometimes called "Muse" or "Inspiration" or "The Place Where Ideas Come From." But whatever its name, this Thing woke up because of this woman and has never slept a wink since.

The Thing drove me to write. I wrote all the time—without exaggeration. On the bus to and from school. In the back of the classroom. At the lunch table. In bed late at night and again early in the morning. I wrote on vacation and later—when I had to get a day job to pay for my writing life—I even wrote during working hours.

I was praised and prized for my writing. And today I make a very good living and provide a wonderful life for my family from my writing. And all of that—the writing and the living—I owe very specifically to that woman.

The woman, of course, is you. Your constant support and praise, even when I felt like I was crap and worthless and my writing even less than that, kept me pushing to be better. And if I am ever good, it will be because of you.

I heard that you were sick. I lost my mother two years ago to cancer—I wouldn't wish it on anyone, ever. And though I am not a doctor and could never do anything to make you well again, I wanted to tell you that I hope for your recovery. And I want you to understand how pivotal you are in my life. The oh-so-famous Dieudonne St. Pierre would never have written even a grocery list had it not been for you.

Thank you. Thank you thank you thank you. I wish you hope and sunshine and love and goodness.

Sincerely,

Donnie

"Surprised again, aren't you, Jo?" Ed grins his whole face full, as he used to say. "Look at your face!" he says. "Shock and awe!"

I'm crying. Big, soft tears falling down the sides of my face and dropping onto my horrible hospital gown. But I'm also smiling. And it's not because of the compliments in the letter. It's because I remember suddenly what good people there are in the world. If I just watched the news all day, I would be forgiven for thinking that the world is a terrible place full of terrible people doing terrible things to each other. But that's not true at all. In fact, it's actually a lie. Donnie and probably every one of my students is likely living a low-middle life right now somewhere in America and being basically good. That's the truth of humanity. Most people are just being good and getting on with getting on.

Wow, what a jolt. Donnie was an incredible student. Quiet and at times morose, but deep and full of curiosity and wanting to *know*. He has become such an incredible writer—and I cannot take credit for *any* of it. But it seems to him that I at least provided the initial kick in the pants that he needed to bring his gift out of hiding and share it with the world.

And share he did: he won the Pulitzer Prize!

I guess I can take credit for that now, too.

"Ha!" Ed laughs at me. "You old—" I cut him off with a glare before he can finish.

Chapter Three

A SUNRISE IS A kind of hope: the hope that even as something terrible happens, some beautiful thing is shattered or some wonderful time crashes to an end and the clock halts, that no matter what happens the sun will keep rising like it always does, like it has for all of human history, and likely will for the rest of it.

I suspect that humanity will meet its end long before the sun does.

But when I see the sun rise like I do this morning, I can have some hope. A little slice of hope pie just for me. The hope that I will make it through this, live long enough to look back. Because that's all I want. I want to live *long enough* to be able to look *back enough*.

With a heart full of hope and veins full of methadone I drift off again.

When I wake, the sea is lit from underneath, a trick of the sunlight coming through a blanket of gray clouds. I stare and imagine what it must be like to stand on those waters and look down.

"You've got a visitor," Maude chirps from the door. I turn away from my view of the sea, my heart still full of hope, and there is my North Star, Abigail. My hope is rewarded.

I was so angry with Rachel when she got pregnant. I knew the baby would ruin her life, destroy her chance to get into Harvard and finish her law degree and move to New York and be a great attorney like she always dreamed of.

She majored in business instead. Got a job for a computer firm and did great. Just finished her MBA last year and is now a Junior VP for acquisitions. So, she proved me wrong.

But more important: her baby girl is here.

Right now I cannot imagine my life without this wonderful little person. Especially right now, today, this moment. Feeling sick and wishing I were dead and there she comes bounding into my room with her locks of red-blond hair (I never knew who the father was, but suspected Eric Fielding once I saw that hair) and her smile and all the single decade of her happiness and wisdom shining in her gray-green eyes.

Her hair is like a sunrise. And her eyes are like the sea where it bubbles and washes against a rocky shore along a shallow shelf.

My god! She is perfect. I thank god and the universe and every deity that ever was or will be that I got the chance to meet this girl.

Abigail. My granddaughter.

She runs over all arms and legs and pigtails like something out of an old movie and tries to hug me over the safety rail of the bed. Frustrated, she tries to clamber up and over but Maude is there and pulls her back.

"No climbing on the bed, missy," she says, *tsk-tsking*. "Your grandmother isn't strong enough for you to be up there—and neither is the bed."

I want to disagree, but Maude gives me a look that says, *Don't even think about it.*

Abigail crumples into a chair in the corner and crosses her arms, knees drawn up, pouting. And looking as cute as a little kitten. I remember that when Rachel was a little girl and sat pouting like that I'd be furious.

Maude busies herself with some sheets and acts as if she hasn't completely ruined the whole day.

"You've completely ruined my whole day, Maude," I say.

"Mm-hmm," she responds.

Picking up the last of the things, Maude goes to the door and leaves without another word or look, pulling the door gently closed behind her.

Abigail stares at the door for a long moment, her head tilted to one side. Then she turns and gives me the slyest look I've ever seen on another person.

Jumping up, her face lit from the inside with a beaming smile, she practically sprints over to my bed and leaps over the safety rail, snuggling up along my body. I hug her close. She smells so good. All sunshine and flowers and innocence and love.

Oh, god, I think. *Please don't ever let me forget this. Whatever comes next, please don't ever let me forget this tiny moment.*

It's dark, the light from the bathroom playing shadows across the floor. Abigail is gone. The sun is gone. The curtains are drawn. I asked Maude to leave them open, but while I dozed the night orderly must have come in and closed them.

I wish I could walk. I wish I could climb out of this bed and open the blinds. But I'm also afraid. I'm scared I'll discover that behind those blinds is only a blank wall. And that maybe I've died and ended up in hell after all. This antiseptic room with its grotesque shades drawn over a blank wall is all I get from now until eternity.

Hell is a hospital room.

Chapter Four

HONESTLY, I CANNOT IMAGINE a more glorious sunrise than this one. If this were to be my last sunrise, I would welcome it and cherish it, and remember it for as long as I could. There is so much subtlety to it, so much color, so much emotive light and interplay with the water. The sea is so calm this morning as if it knows a storm will come again and it should just take it easy for as long as it can.

As long as... It's a phrase I keep coming back to again and again. I want to live, to love, to *know* as long as I can. As long as possible. As long as the gods and the universe will let me. I want this sunrise to last as long as it can.

I've been up again since before the nautical twilight. Ed was here—not looking at me, but simply staring out through the glass, his back to me—but now he's gone. As soon as the sky began to lighten up, he faded away. I'm incomprehensibly worried I'll never see him again. Which is stupid, because I haven't seen him in over a decade anyway.

It's been a calming morning. The sea is calm. The sunrise tip-toed up and then made a peek-a-boo over the curved horizon. And all along the way, the colors were simply marvelous. Today's sunrise was an ever-changing kaleidoscope that I could never quite focus on or capture. The light and the colors were as elusive as a shadow jumping at sunbeams shining through the trees into a moving car—and I didn't try to capture it. I just watched. I just removed myself from my own mind, danced slowly out away from my body, and did my best to join the starlight in its morning ritual of bathing this little spot of earth where I live in its glow.

Maude will be here in a bit, bringing me my horrid breakfast. But it's all right. It's all right because this particular sunrise—and maybe all the ones that have come before—was so magnificent that nothing could spoil it. The cloudless sky and waveless sea made sure that the spotlight this morning shone solely on the sun as it rose onto the stage of the day.

I sigh, marveling at the simultaneously simple and complex beauty of nature.

I play absently with the seashell necklace.

My mind wanders and settles here and there on nothing in particular. But I am suddenly overwhelmed by smells and sounds and tastes inside my mind, calling up a million indistinct memories, events that may have happened, people I may have known and loved, foods I may have tasted.

Then, suddenly and so strongly: Ed's smell. The raw, sun-kissed-skin smell of him. God, I *miss* that smell. His scent was the thing that made me feel most at home. Snuggled against his chest in the dark of our bedroom, smelling his golden scent, I felt safe and vulnerable at the same time. That little moment, lying with Ed, naked, our bodies as close as our skin and our bones would let us be, that's the moment I want to remember the longest. As long as possible. Forever, even—if I can.

And then the sun is up and it's a gorgeous day and the sunlight is sparkling so brightly off the water that

I have to squint and then close my eyes. And suddenly I'm very tired and feel the strongest need simply to slip back into sleep, to lay there in Ed's arms, smelling Ed's scent, loving and being loved. Drifting off, the two of us, together.

It's almost a shame to wake up again. You know when you're in that half-dream state and you can't remember what you were dreaming, but it was wonderful—and then you drift up out of it (or get jolted out of it) and you keep grasping, trying to remember, trying to clutch at it, to keep it for even just another nanosecond? I love and hate those moments. I hate them for the obvious reasons: I'm being pulled away from something wondrous and wonderful. But I love them because I know (or think—maybe I read it someplace) that if I were not on the verge of waking, I would never even remember that I had been in this fantastic place at all. It would have remained hidden in my subconscious, lurking, waiting until I closed my eyes once more and slept long enough to get back to the place where dreams live.

And I'll be honest: I've never been certain whether dreams are real, or reality a dream. I've never believed in god and religion and all of that strongly enough to be convinced that everything is as it seems and there is a plan for each of us. I'm pretty sure that anything is possible. And I mean absolutely anything.

I could be a character in someone's book, like in that film. Or I could be a simulation or a non-player character in an advanced computer game like Abigail keeps trying to explain to me. Or I could be another being altogether, simply dreaming. And in my dream, I age slowly in this other body, but in this imagined other reality, I have only been asleep for an hour.

Anything is possible. And like any true possibility, all the doors and windows are open.

What door or window would I choose, if I could? Would I choose something different from this? Would I choose something *other*? It's a tempting thought.

But I always circle back to Eddie and Rachel and Abigail: would a different window or door—or choice, really—exclude them? I absolutely could not bear the idea of living a reality that did not include them. In that case, I could imagine that I would break.

Oh, god: not to mention all the other wonderful people I've met along the way! *Good lord!* Okay, I'll stop the exercise now. Too bleak.

And then the circle closes: my life *is* bleak.

Who am I trying to convince that everything will be okay? My daughter and granddaughter? Eddie? *Myself?* There's no convincing to be done: either I recover or I die. There are no other roads. And the way I feel sometimes I'm not sure I'll make the turn down the first road. And that thought fills me with panic and anxiety and regret. No matter how many pages I fill in my journal with lists of things for which I am grateful (always on top: Ed, Rachel, Abigail, the sunrise), I still can't seem to shake this thought that I could have and should have done more, become more, *loved* more. And if I feel that way, is it true? Are we reduced to our emotions when assaying our lives? What worth is there in my home on the Bay? Or the things in it? What worth is there in my degrees? Am I more valuable because of an award I received? Does even Donnie's wonderful card really validate what I've done and who I've been?

I'm afraid. I'm afraid I will leave this world this very instant without having done and been and loved all that I could.

But even more than that I'm afraid of simply dying. Of the show being over. No more episodes. Not another minute of dialogue. Just a camera pan to the setting sun out over the ocean as the credits start to roll.

I am *not* ready for the credits to start rolling just yet!

I have not drunk in enough of Abigail's fresh youthful joy.

I have not told Rachel enough times how proud I am of her.

I have not dreamed enough about my life with Ed.

I need a little more time. I need a little more focus.

And right this second I need a little more methadone.

Maude is back. Something's wrong with her. I get the feeling it doesn't have to do with me. But I can tell by her posture. She doesn't usually say much to me, but today she is absolutely stoic. I wonder what has put her in such a state. She's always so *even*. Never jubilant. Never furious. Never full of grief. Just a nice warm *middle* kind of way. In spite of her being the source of most of my consternation these days, I want to comfort her.

I'm suddenly unsure whether our relationship is such that I can even ask.

"Maude," I say quietly.

She snaps her head my way and I can tell in her bloodshot eyes and intense-but-vacant stare that something really horrible has happened.

I watch her silently as her mouth works itself into a shallow smile. I can tell it's painful work. It looks as if it takes all of her strength and willpower to turn her mouth up just a tiny bit at the corners and to soften her eyes just a little. And then I realize that she is doing all of this hard internal work entirely for me and for me alone.

My heart aches. For *her*.

I raise my left hand, reaching feebly across the distance between us. She is bent over, putting some things away inside the table next to the bed. She straightens her back and reaches out with her own hand. Her skin is dry and cool and she clasps my hand, giving it a brief squeeze. Then she lets go, clears her throat, and starts stacking dirty sheets and clothes between one bent arm and her chest.

"Dinner will be along shortly," she says. She bustles to the door and pauses, her free hand resting on the knob. She turns to look at me and the intense glare is there, defiant. "Thank you," she says. Then she leaves.

"What was that about, do you think?" Ed is tapping out a tattoo with his fingers on the table next to the bed. He does that when he's worried. It always gets under my skin.

"I don't know," I say. "But it has to be terrible."

"Has to be," he says. "She's never like that." He sighs deeply.

I nod my head in agreement.

"Stop that!" I snap at him and he quits his little finger drumming. "I hope she's going to be all right," I say, looking at the door.

"Well, I'm pretty sure she has the same hope for you," Ed says. He strolls over to the door, peeking through the small window into the hallway. "Isn't that something?" he says. "We always look outward with our concerns. Never inward. I've never said, 'I hope I'm going to be all right.' It sounds ridiculous even thinking it."

"I don't know," I say. "Maybe it's what we *should* be doing."

"What do you mean?" he asks.

"Maybe we should have hoped for more for *us*. Maybe I should be hoping for more for myself now. Maybe I should take better care of my *own* emotions and psyche."

"Maybe," he says. "And if you did, what would you hope for? Wait!" he says, clapping his hands. "Let's play a game!" He hops back over to my bed and sits on the end of it. "I hope I get to see the Rays play in the World Series!" he cries, punching me gently in the leg. He knows I never cared for *baseball.*

"You old fool," I chide. "First of all, never happened in your lifetime. Second, that's the worst kind of thing to hope for."

"Okay, miss higher-than-thou. Show this old fool how to hope." He smiles and crosses his arms across his chest.

"I don't have many hopes," I say.

"But not *no* hope!" Ed slaps his knee, bending over to cackle. I'm not amused—I never liked Tolkien anyway.

I glare at him for a moment. "I hope," I say at last. "That I get to live a little longer."

Ed blows a raspberry. "Now you're just being morbid," he says.

"I also hope," I say, ignoring him. "That I get to spend more time with Rachel and Abigail."

"Well," he says, nodding. "That's something worth hoping for."

"And finally—" I begin.

"Finally? That's it? Three hopes?" Ed exclaims.

"It's like Aladdin. Three wishes," I say.

"Fine. Write a book someday: *The Three Hopes*." He laughs.

"And finally," I say again. "I hope I get to watch the sun rise tomorrow."

"Now that's a hope I can go to sleep to at night," he says.

My thoughts exactly.

Ed walks right up to the windows and fades in the late afternoon light streaming in from outside. He's gone again for now. And it's okay. My heart is so full of hope right now I feel like it might burst.

Three little hopes: to *live* and to *spend time* and to *watch*.

That's all I ask for.

I can't wait for another sunrise.

Chapter Five

I WISH EDDIE WERE here. I mean *for real* here. I miss his nonsense. His *jibber jabber*. The endless spill of his words. Eddie would make me stop feeling so sorry for myself. He would know just what to say. He always did.

"You know, Josie," he would say. "You can't stay in bed all damn day. I mean, look out there! Look at all that water. Who's gonna drink it? That taciturn battle-axe of a nurse? *Me*? C'mon, Josie, aren't you thirsty? I'll go grab us a couple of straws..."

But he's not here. He left me a long time ago.

I didn't think I'd live long after Eddie died. I thought, *That's it: heart broken, life over*. And for a while it seemed like I might not make it, that I might follow him after all. But it was he himself who got me through it. Him and his words.

I sat for eight days on the big gray sectional in our bay-front home and read every one of his letters and cards. Then I spent another two weeks reading through decades of emails and text messages.

And then for a week I just cried.

I hardly slept. And a month had gone by and I was still alive.

"The sun will rise tomorrow," he wrote in his last letter to me. "And I want you to see it for me. However many sunrises you get to witness after I'm gone, I want you to remember them all and I want you to tell me about them when you see me again. In every little detail."

And that's what I've lived on for the last dozen or so years: the sun will rise tomorrow. And I will see it. And I will remember it. For Eddie.

When we met, Eddie was just out of the Navy after six years as a small boat driver (a coxswain, or "cock-sun" as he said it) for what Eddie called the Brown Water Navy, which apparently is the nickname for sailors who drive boats in the rivers and swamps of the world. He loved boats and I loved beaches and we both loved the sea and each other. It was a good match—no, a *great* match. We spent the rest of our lives chasing the ocean.

We moved to Florida and he worked the waters as a boat captain and I worked the local children as a teacher and we had a really good life. We made enough money, we had nice enough things. But mostly, we had each other and the sea.

"Josie," he would whisper in the dark. "Josie, wake up." I always hated the morning, but I had grown to like his little ritual. He sat there on the edge of the bed, a steaming cup of coffee in his hand (*his* coffee; he would bring me mine much later), grin on his face, his other hand resting on my thigh.

"Sunrise in three minutes," he said. He always checked his almanac or some such record and knew the exact time of every sunrise.

Wrapping my blanket around me, we tiptoed through the living room and out onto the deck together, both of us looking east across the low marshes. There was a row of beachfront homes (a little out of our price range) and beyond them the big Atlantic Ocean, stretching across to Africa.

The houses were still black silhouettes, the world here along this bit of coast still hiding in the night, but way out there, miles distant, the sky was lightening. A thin band of gold appeared and shot across the horizon from left to right as far as I could see. I forgot to be grumpy and tired—I even forgot to breathe.

That instant, the one between night and day, left me in awe every time.

People always speak about the creeping dawn, the idea that there is a gradual transition from night to day. But it's a lie. The word daybreak is more accurate: the night disappears with a whipcrack of starlight, the sun slicing a bright, brutal curve along the seam of the earth and sky, cutting the night away without transition, peeling back the blue-black sky and pouring light in.

I think you can only see this on the ocean or only on the east-facing coast. Sunsets are misleading. They're gradual. They fade. They gasp dying breaths like old people clinging to the last moments of existence and then slowly drift into darkness.

But not the sunrise.

A sunrise is bold, urgent. It cries out, *There are things to do! Get up! Crow, rooster! Type, writer! Drive, cowboy! Hoist, sailor!*

And then the urgency fades as the sun quickly pulls itself up over the edge of the globe. Day comes, and with it the heat and the bustle and the brightness.

And then I would squeeze Eddie's hand while he sipped his coffee with the other. That one little moment. A smile in our hearts. A shared reminder that today the sun rose and under its light two people got to share another day together, to love each other a little longer.

Slipping back into bed, I would drift to sleep and dream of a sunrise that never ended, that gold and blood orange glow throbbing for eternity.

This morning the sun rose slowly. I didn't want it to, but the sun and her sisters do what they do. I wanted it to snap to attention, to brighten my day. Because here on this bed in this room in this hospital all is dim.

Rachael called to tell me she couldn't come this weekend. Something came up with work and she had to cram all weekend to get some document or other finished. And that was on Monday. Today's Friday and I've heard nothing in the interim. Days go by like this, sometimes. Sometimes we just don't communicate with people. Sometimes we cocoon and we myope on our narrow and very personal private lives.

I'm pretty sure that sometimes we also simply binge on Netflix.

I admit it: I do it too. I ignore texts and emails and phone calls. Even now. Even when I'm lying here in a cancer hospital dying, I sometimes ignore the people who care about me. People who want me to win, to survive, to beat this thing and keep on living. How long? What, another twenty years? Maybe?

God, twenty years would be amazing. I'm guessing before this treatment is over I'll be thinking twenty minutes is worth the effort. Just to have another half-hour with someone you love. What wouldn't we give for that?

And there I am going on all morose again. I spent every day for over thirty years side-by-side with a man I knew in every intimate detail. And I'll tell you this: there were definitely times when I wanted just to be *away* from him for twenty minutes.

My goodness, but he could make me hot! Piss me off like no one else. Make me mad for no reason and then laugh at me when I raised my hackles. Let me give you a little advice: laughing at an angry person is a bad idea. A wise man once said something like the best thing to do if you meet the devil is to laugh in his face. I'm pretty sure if you did that you'd be stuck with a pitchfork and tossed in fiery brimstone before you could say, "Wait a second!"

So, I'll just leave it at that. Because I'm pretty pissed off right now too. Not a peep from Rachel since Monday and no chance of seeing her and Abby this weekend. Crap. Just, *crap*.

"Good morning, Jo!" Maude sings from the door. I am so caught up in my anger I didn't even hear her open it. She's got that maniac morning smile on her face. The one that says, "Everything's going to be okay!" on the lips and teeth and, "Everything's falling apart around me!" in the eyes.

Wow. How does she do it? And why am I so stubbornly selfish that I can't?

I don't smile back.

"Oh, Jo," she chides. "Don't be so down-in-the-dumps." Somehow her smile actually reaches her eyes this time. Maybe it's schadenfreude. Maybe she can see how crap-damn mad I am. So mad I'm making up the stupidest curse word combos in my mind.

I realize quite suddenly that all the foul language running through my head is in Eddie's voice. Eddie the foul-mouthed sailor. I never really curse out loud. Then I hear him start to laugh. And he keeps on laughing so hard and so hysterically that I snort a couple of times and then I'm off laughing and Jo looks at me sideways and then *she's* laughing.

Then I scrunch up my stomach and hunch forward and start coughing like the dickens.

The laughing slows down. It stops. My eyes are wet.

God, I miss Eddie.

"It's going to be okay," Maude says. She puts my breakfast in front of me and I can see she's swiped a cup of plain Greek yogurt—my favorite and *impossible* to come by in this place.

I heave out a great after-laughter sigh.

"Thanks, Maude," I tell her. "Really. Thank you."

She gently touches my hand and smiles.

"Enjoy the sunrise," she says. "Sometimes they last long enough to make us believe they'll never end."

She stands there, one hand resting on my hand, staring out the window at the sun coming up over the water. The colors are the same, but different. Brilliantly mixing shades of red, yellow, and blue to form a palette only the greatest painters could dream of. Every day, the sun does this. Every day, something subtly different than the day before and yet somehow more perfect, more amazing, more grand.

Suddenly, it's okay that Rachael's not coming. Because she has important things to do. She is the main character in the story of her life and I cannot fathom the array of things she has to contend with every day. I can remember being stressed about some school-related thing or another in the past. And I remember believing that no one could understand the pressure I was under. Whether it was grading papers or preparing for school events, I was at times a very busy lady.

But the honest truth is that there were people more and also less stressed than I was. Just like there are people who are better people than I am. And also worse.

And I can forgive Rachael for choosing work over me this weekend, because it's the life *she* is living. And besides, forgiveness is for the *forgiver*, not the forgiven. It's simply to make me feel better and to take responsibility for the things I can control and let go of those I can't.

I reach over and take my phone out of the bedside table drawer. I open it up and send Rachael a message.

I know you have a ton on your plate. Get your work done and try to find some time for yourself and for Abby. And breathe. I love you.

A few moments later, she texts back. A simple red heart. It's enough. I spend the next twenty minutes watching the slow sunrise and eating small spoonfuls of the yogurt. It's one of the best morning's I've had in a long time.

Chapter Six

THE SUNRISE DIDN'T EVEN happen today. At least, not for me. I'm not even in my room—I'm in the *cutting room*, as I like to call it. It's where they make me *feel* worse while trying to make me *be* better.

Ah, crap. This is the reality of this disease. This pain. This nausea. I can't even think. The suffering is overwhelming and I just want it to end, to stop; whether that means I stop along with it is unimportant. The important thing is for this feeling to stop.

I give up.

Eddie, do you hear me? This is my "me too" moment: I give up! Just like you did. I lasted longer than you did. I started fighting right from the start. But I can't do this anymore. I can't go through this one more second. It's too much.

I know: I need to keep fighting. *But to hell with this pain and to hell with you for not being here to help me through this!*

I'm irrational. I think I'm literally losing my mind at this point. My chest feels like Maude is kneeling on it, and others keep climbing onto her back, building a tower of nurses that keep upping the pressure, crushing me.

I can't breathe.

"I can't breathe!" I yell.

I don't think anyone can hear me. When I scream, the clear plastic mouth mask just fogs up and a wheezing whisper squeezes between my lips.

Someone adjusts the mask over my face.

No one holds my hand.

Where is Eddie?

"Where is Ed!" I yell.

I feel at once groggy and acutely aware of pain. My whole existence is simply pain. I can't communicate. I can't lift my arms. I can't even turn my head.

But I can *feel*. And what I feel is so bad, so jab-a-screwdriver-into-my-thigh bad that I don't know how I can even continue being conscious.

Then the nausea is suddenly too much and I vomit into the face mask and puke pools around my mouth and nose and I start gagging and coughing and *where the hell is everyone*!

I'm going to drown here in my own stomach bile. I just know it. This is it. I won't die from cancer after all—I'll just drown in my own green vomit.

Then someone is there, pulling the mask away and wiping me and opening my slack mouth, and cleaning it out. And someone else is pumping something into my IV line and then the pain takes a step or two away, giving me some breathing room, and my eyelids grow heavy and I'm out of here.

Later, lying in my bed in my room, the curtains still open and the daylight fading, I don't feel much better. But anything I feel now is better than how I felt earlier.

It's this all-over pain that is getting to me. The cancer is pretty localized—it's all in my chest and abdomen. But the pain is absolutely everywhere. My toes ache. My fingers feel arthritic. My knees and elbows throb. My neck is killing me. And I have what is probably the worst migraine I've ever had.

Add to that my nausea. I remember the first time Ed took me out on a small fishing boat. We were behind the barrier island for most of the way and then we rounded the point and the sea was there to meet us and suddenly we were pitching up and down and rolling side to side—and then also yawing—and the combined motions were like a malevolent dance whose sole purpose was to haul your stomach from *inside* your body to *outside*. And the process was so violent that I was sure I was puking actual stomach tissue and not just the lobster-and-grits breakfast we had enjoyed an hour before.

This feeling I have now is way worse.

I want to die. And then I think about what that means and I absolutely do *not* want to die. I want to see Abigail again. I want to see another sunrise—because this morning's was crap.

But lying here in my bed, the world outside gone dark, it's hard to imagine that the sun will reappear.

"Where's Rache?" Ed asks from the chair. "I've seen little Abbie running around, so Rachel must be here."

He *knows* she's been here. But she won't come in. Won't deal with any of this. Some days, I think, she just comes to the hospital and walks around, peeking into other patients' windows or slowly ambling through the gardens. She thinks this whole thing is harder on her than it is on me. And that's okay. It's how we're built. We are the stars of our own personal movies.

But I wish this idea wouldn't keep her from coming to see me. I have so much I still want to tell her. I want to leave her behind remembering how proud I am of her, how much I love her, how much joy she brought to my life, how much I don't give a crap that she had a kid so young. I want her to remember me fondly, not with a host of small regrets that add up to an uncomfortable, "Well, my relationship with my mom was...complicated" kind of thing.

Nobody wants that, I suppose.

But anyway, that's where I am. Wish in one hand, crap in the other. Days like today, I'm convinced not only that the crap hand will fill up first, but that there is in fact only crap in the other hand too.

"Where's Rache?" Ed asks again. But his voice is fading. "Where's Rache?" he repeats. And repeats, fading into quiet.

"Grammy?" Abigail is standing next to the bed, watching me stare at a faded

Ed and a shadowy seashore through the window. I wipe back the tears.

"Hi, sweetie," I say. "Come over here." And she comes to me and hugs me and I'm okay for the moment. "Tell me about your week," I say. "What amazing adventures did you have?"

"Nothing special," she says. She doesn't understand that to me every little part of her and her life is special. A miracle.

"Well," I say. "Tell me about the not-so-special things you did this week."

And as she does, she carries me away from my pain, my regret, my fear of dying—even if only for a little while.

Chapter Seven

WHAT MOST PEOPLE DON'T realize—what *I* never realized—is that dying is a process. Like a sunrise or a sunset, it has been happening, slowly, all night or all day long. The moment the sun rises over the sea the clock is ticking to the point where it will set. And while it seems on the one hand that when we're born we start growing into the person we will become, the truth is that we're just moving inevitably toward our eventual death. Every moment that passes belongs to death. Every moment is one that we will never get back again. And that is why I feel so compelled to make the most of whatever moments I have left.

When Eddie was dying—from the cancer, not just regular dying like normal people—I sometimes went through the five stages of grief all in a day. I'm not sure I even realized it at the time. I was so caught up in trying to unpack everything that I hardly knew what day it was. But at some point Ed was in the hospital—this same hospital, in fact—dying. And I felt more alone then than I do now that he's gone.

Anyway, I've settled into the final stage as gracefully as I can. I still miss him. I still talk to him even. But it's not the daily roller coaster that I was on back then.

I'd wake up in the morning and think that Eddie was just off on some trip. That he'd gone to visit an old navy buddy I either I'd forgotten about it or he'd forgotten to tell me. I'd make coffee, watch the early morning sky (I missed every single sunrise while Eddie was in the hospital), and scroll through the news on my phone. Maybe I'd answer a text or an email. Sometimes I'd call my friend, Sandy, and just talk about things—but not about Ed and cancer. And my mornings would be pretty good. I became an expert in packing all the emotions I was feeling about Eddie's sickness into a small, dark corner of my mind.

Around midday, the emotions would all come bubbling to the surface and I would become so furious with Ed that he wasn't fighting hard enough. Somehow this whole thing was *his* fault. *He* was the one who'd gotten cancer after all. And I would scream and cry at the same time, although I never thought that was even possible. I threw my wallet and a snack and a water bottle and a paperback into my purse, slamming-stuffing each thing in as I said some unmemorable thing or another about Ed, and then went out to the car, flung my purse across into the passenger seat, slammed the door and just gripped the steering wheel, rocking forward and backward and sobbing and yelling. Then I'd go back inside and try to calm down because I was in no condition to drive and certainly not in the right frame of mind to visit my *dying husband* in the hospital.

Eventually, I would go see him. Spend an hour or two sitting by his bed, playing cribbage, or giving him updates on the world outside. And then the pain would come and he would mash the button for more *relief* and the methadone would ease him into sleep and I would sit a little longer before heading back home, emotionally exhausted.

By dinnertime, I'd be making all sorts of promises. And if making promises to the gods didn't work, I'd drive right back to the hospital and shout in Eddie's face absolutely *begging* him not to die. I told the doctor over and over how much money I could come up with for experimental treatments that weren't covered by our insurance. (He was doing all he could, he promised.) I asked Rachel to come more often, to bring Abigail by more often. I asked some of Eddie's navy buddies to visit (they never did). But mostly, I sat alone by the water (either at home or at the hospital) pleading with Nature, with the sun, with the sea to *please-please-please* let Eddie be well again.

After supper, I would sit by myself on the deck with the sun setting somewhere off behind me and the sea in front of me darkening into black and drink an entire bottle of red wine. And in those interminable hours, I would face the dark night of the soul, picturing Ed lying in an open casket, imagining my life without him. I could not fathom what that would even look like. What would I do all day? Who would I tell my troubles to? Who would play cards with me and take me out to dinner every Friday night? And, oh, my god, who would make me laugh every single day? I was going to be alone. For the rest of my life. *Forever.* And the love of my life, my dream man, would never wake me up again before dawn just to watch the sun rise over the sea. I simply could not bear it. And I knew, I absolutely knew, that *I* would die the moment *he* did.

And finally, crawling into bed at night, still tipsy and teary-eyed, I would close my eyes and breathe deeply and reach out to run my hand over the empty place where Eddie should be lying next to me. And in doing that, I could catch a glimpse of us together, a little look back through the window of time to when we were younger and the idea that one day one of us would die was ridiculous. In that small moment between being awake and being asleep, I could see my life unfolding in an *After Eddie* kind of way. I could hold onto the memories, feel the love, know the truth of our bond and understand that there might be a little bit of life left for me in a world without him. That I would still have Rachel and Abigail. That I could spend time reminding Abby what a great man her grandfather was. And that—if I lived long enough—I could share all that I had learned simply loving and by being loved.

And I would drift off to sleep, at peace for the moment. And in that brief respite—maybe seven hours or so—I would truly rest. Until the next day brought the cycle again.

Rachel can't stop crying.

"Please don't cry, sweetie. Not now, not here. You can cry when you leave."

"That's just the thing, Mama," she whispers. "When I'm not here, I don't think about it. I don't think about you lying here, sick, frail—*dying*."

"Good!" I reassure her. "This isn't the way I want you to think about me, anyway. Please, Rache, *please* don't remember me like this."

I look at her sitting there and all I can see is my little girl. And I can't bear to see her sad. Angry is okay. She can be mad all she wants. She certainly deserves to be angry about what is happening. But it hurts worse than cancer to see her sad.

"Today's your birthday, Rachel. And it's an amazing day. When you came into the world, I thought my heart would break. That I wouldn't be able to bear the beauty and joyous wonder of your brand new existence. And later, I felt like I would just fall apart. I think your dad put it best. He said: 'I'm just so goddamned sad that I'll have to leave her someday, that I won't live forever and be able to kiss her or hug her or smell her hair—that one day I won't get to experience that anymore.' And you know what I told him?"

Rachel is sobbing now.

"I said: 'But *she* will be able to remember all of that. She'll carry you with her—in her heart—after you're gone. After we're *both* gone.'"

"Oh, Jesus, Mama!" Rachel barked. "*Please* lighten the mood." And she laughs hard and long and she reaches over the safety rail to hug me and I feel like she might be okay after all. And maybe, just maybe, I will be too.

"Well, today's your birthday. It's *your* day. Every year, every birthday—heck, every time the sun comes up—is a new beginning for everyone; today you can start everything anew."

She pulls away and walks toward the windows, her back to me.

"Do you remember when I was little and I couldn't sleep?" she asks.

I smile. "Of course—you'd come crawl into bed with us."

"Snug as a bug in a rug," Ed says suddenly, smiling at Rachel from across the room. I stare him silent.

"That's right," Rachel says. "I'd come into your bed. It was so nice and warm and *safe*."

She turns and takes a step back toward me and I can see her body has tightened up. She's getting angry again.

"But at some point," she continues. "I don't know, maybe I was ten, you got tired of me coming into the room. You would snap at me and tell me if I didn't go to bed *this instant* I'd see the worst side of you."

"Oh, *god*," I say, my hand coming up to my chest, clutching the seashell necklace. It was cold and not at all comforting. I suddenly remember saying that so clearly.

"So, after a while," she says. "I stopped coming. But the *need* to come to you didn't go away. Just the *permission*. I still woke up from terrible dreams, or lay in bed not able to sleep and I just stayed there, thinking about how you would react if I came to your room. How loud you might yell at me. And I always wondered what that worst side of you would look like. And in the end, I decided I didn't want to find out."

She takes another step and her focus shifts to look somewhere behind me. I wonder suddenly if she can see her father there with us.

"I'd forgotten about it until I came in here and saw you lying in that god-awful bed." She's crying now. "It makes me so sad, so squeezed up tight inside." She clenches both fists to show me what that feels like.

"I'm so sorry, honey," I mutter. "I can't change it. I can't take it back."

"I don't want you to take it back. I just want to crawl into bed with you, Mama! I just want to be little again!"

I stretch my arms out and she runs over to me like a Hallmark holiday and hugs me and smothers her snotty face into my neck and sobs and shakes.

I love every second of it.

I try to hold on to all of it. Her smell. The feeling of her arms and head and chest against me. Her warmth. Her love and her pain. I don't want to forget this beautiful girl. I don't want to lose her—for her to lose me.

"And I was always so pissed at Papa," she mumbles into my neck, sniffing back her tears. "I still am. He just sat there next to you in that bed and let you push me away and he did *nothing*."

I look over Rachel's shoulder at Ed standing in the corner. He looks down at his shoes.

"That wasn't his way, sweetie," I try.

"Fuck his way, Mama!"

"Honey...," I try to soothe.

She pulls away and it's agony for me, the cold hospital room air filling the warm space she occupied.

"Jesus, Mama, I'm sorry," she says, wiping her eyes with the backs of her hands.

"It's okay. Everything's okay."

"No, Mama. *Nothing's* okay. But it doesn't matter." She lets out a huge sigh and starts picking up her things.

"Are you going?" I ask. I know the answer. I wonder what excuse she will give.

"Yes. I...," she looks back at the corner where Ed was standing. He's not there anymore. "It's just too much emotion today, Mama. I'm sorry."

Well, at least she's honest.

"I love you, Rache," I say. "I will always love you."

"I know, Mama. I love you too," she says, but it's a throwaway line. And she walks over to me all business-like and bends down to kiss me on the head like a child. She smiles and walks over to the door. "I'll bring Abby next weekend," she says over her shoulder. Then she's out the door and gone and I'm alone again.

Chapter Eight

AFTER THE SEA AT sunrise, after the long day, the twilight comes just before the night. At sea, the twilight lingers. The sun seems to set for hours. After passing its zenith, our yellow-white star drops slowly to the horizon, gently burying itself in the water. That's when you see all the colors. The sky shifts from its pale blue to a kaleidoscope of everything until the fabled "green flash" followed by the shift from orange to red to purple to ink. And then the twilight.

As before dawn, the evening twilight seems to last, bright enough to read by, even now as I lay here. But unlike the pre-dawn background glow in the sky—which seems to promise everything, all the potential of the coming day—the evening twilight is grasping at a light that is slipping, drifting into the blackest black.

The metaphor of sunsets for fading life is apt: we reach and we grasp and we cling, but the light fades inevitably toward darkness. And we want it to be this way. We hope for it to be this way. Because the other way is unfair. The other way is the child killed by a reckless driver, the young soldier shot in war, the baby not fully formed and clinging only for a moment to all the wonder and beauty that life exposes us to, that life promises us. It's the candle snuffed out by a brisk puff of wind. The lamp switched off. The call dropped.

We want—we *need*—the twilight. It gives us just long enough to summarize. Just enough time to reflect, to think about what it meant to live, to have known others and shared in their experiences. To have loved.

And it is during this twilight that we remember everything. Absolutely everything we have ever done and everyone we have ever known comes rushing in and bursting with light and our hearts swell and we know—for one instant—pure joy! Pure happiness. Pure living.

And then night comes. The light goes out. And we know nothing more.

Lying here in the dim light of the strip of LEDs across the bottom of the wall, I can't remember my first day here. How long has it been? I feel like I've somehow crossed a line, a point of no return, that means I'm stuck here until my body gives up the ghost and I join my ancestors in the astral plane.

Or something like that.

I hope when I *do* go—and not today, for goodness sakes!—that either there is something warm and bright and beautiful waiting for me, some wholly new experience full of oxytocin and joy and *understanding*—or nothing. I want something amazing or I want eternal blackness. The deep sleep. The long goodnight.

Now I remember—skin cancer biopsy followed by blood in my urine. Some x-rays and then WHAM!

"You've got cancer," the doctor said oh-so-matter-of-factly.

Cancer.

It's just a part of our human dialogue now.

So common: "Oh, my aunt has cancer."

A headline: "Steve Jobs just died of cancer."

A slogan: "My wife had breast cancer—and beat it!"

A finality: "The cancer took my husband."

Cancer.

"The prognosis isn't good," I say out loud.

"It's not in your control," Eddie says. He's got his back to me, looking out at the sea through the big windows.

"The hell it isn't, Ed! I'm not going to give up like you did. I'm going to fight this thing. I'm going to *win*!"

I can see his head drop, imagine his eyes closing. His shoulders sag as he sighs.

"What *is* in your control," he says, "is how you handle it all. How you finish. How you go."

And then he's gone. And I'm left thinking about what he said. How *am* I going to finish? How *am* I going to go? Part of me wants to be defiant—I will *not* go gentle into that good night, thank you very much! But what good does it do to rant and rage against the inevitable? Neither do I want simply to lie down and let Death sort of scrape me off the ground and slide me limp into his little bag of bones. No, I want to finish this life doing *something*.

But what?

And for how long? How much time do I have? Do we ever really know? I could leave life this instant—how does knowing that inform what I think and do? And even if I knew—had either some vague timeline (six months?) or something more certain (February 10th?)—would it make any difference? If I died tonight, would I be satisfied that I had done *something* with the time I had been allotted? Was teaching kids enough? Was loving Ed enough? Was creating life enough? Will any of it ever be enough? And what is *enough* anyway?

Am *I* enough?

I'm just going to lie here until the sun comes up. I just want to see that mysteriously relentless thing happen once more. How can every sunrise be so different? How can Nature produce such emotive and unique art so consistently? If I could do what the sunrise does *just once* in my life, I would have achieved the ultimate in human effort. But it's impossible. Not even childbirth comes close.

The sunrise is simply too incredible.

And the sea at sunrise doubly so.

And none of that matters anyway, because here it comes. I'm suddenly jittery all over, shivering, trembling, anticipating. The background light has come up just enough that I *know*. It's an animal knowing, an understanding that has come with time, and patience, and observing.

Here comes the sun!

Chapter Nine

FIRST, THERE IS JUST faint purple haziness. It's the night being pushed back, not too quickly, but steadily, by the burning hand of the sun. You can feel it emerging, pushing, expanding, *rising* out of the sea. There's an energy, a *pulse* to it. Like the sun is alive. Like it's a throbbing, beating thing wanting—demanding—to *be*. To exist. To enter. To consume.

It is all-powerful.

It is exactly 6:28 on a beautiful, partly-cloudy Tuesday.

The clouds are a blessing. They are high and stratus-y. And they take the sunlight, the reds and oranges, and yellows, and mute them and stretch them out like cotton candy across the sky.

The sun isn't actually up yet. I can see it while it is still below the horizon because it's refracted. And as it comes up, it looks wider, fatter, like it's ready to ooze egg-yolk orange magma out into the sea. Raise up an island nation, maybe. Sounds like a beautiful creation myth. And it looks bigger at sunrise than it does later when it's higher in the sky.

And there! *A green flash*! I clap my hands together.

Ha! So it's true after all. I'll have to tell Eddie when I see him.

Suddenly, I'm so confused that I blink my eyes. There are three suns along the horizon. They look like bright shining crosses, like angelic haloes.

Are they shimmering at me? Waving at me? *Beckoning* me? I can feel their tug, strong, pulling me out of my body, out of the hospital, out of the world.

I feel like I'm holding tightly to everything and that the three haloed stars are commanding me simply to let go, release my grip, stop struggling. I let out a shuddering breath and sink back into my pillow, unaware that I had been stretched up and reaching toward the sun.

The three suns pull together again into one and as it keeps coming up the sun becomes too bright to look at and I have to close my eyes.

Behind my eyelids: the burned-in image of the most incredible sunrise I have ever seen.

Things are not going well. I'm in the cutting room and there's a flurry of activity and they're moving to put that mask over my face and there are beeps and low, fast conversations. I try to stay calm, try to breathe, but my chest feels heavy like a crushing weight is bearing down on it. Then here comes the mask and the funny smell and the gradual easiness and fading.

Has the sun set? Is it night? Was that fantastic sun-birth this morning the last I would ever see?

"Remember it," Eddie says. He squeezes my hand gently. "Don't you forget even one little detail. Tell me about it. Tell me everything."

I smile. "I love you," I say to him. His smile tells me everything he needs to say.

My eyes are closed, but the sun is so bright I can see the rippling heat along its edges. The yellow-white eye of the solar system is opening up and staring at everything, watching everything, remembering everything. If the sun could remember all that it has seen, what would it know of me?

Would it know how much and how deeply I loved and was loved? Would it know the tragedy and the triumph and the deep joy that comes from creating life?

Would it remember me in every fine detail as I remember it?

Oh, Eddie: *This is how I see the sea at sunrise...*

The Sea at Sunrise

Watch how my heart disrupts the ink
Of darkest waves in cloudless sky
I rise again and later sink
And in between the caring glow
Of rays cast over all beneath
In defiance of the dark
And all my sparkling halo's wreath
Raises high all hopes and dreams
See how the sailor turns her cheek
To soak her skin in golden rays
She'll meet her end and yet still seek
The quiet purpose of her course
Guided by my noon site light
And driving with a purpose, on
Sailing off in starry night
Until she is no more

I am the sea at sunrise
I am the the bright dawn spark
I am the blaze in every sky
I am the heavens' heart

—Dieudonne St. Pierre

Epilogue

Jacksonville Tribune—Obituaries

Josephine Dunsten Kerner (neé Wilson), a school teacher who was instrumental in helping thousands of disadvantaged children, died Sep. 23 of cancer, her family said. She was 75.

An elementary teacher for almost half a century, Mrs. Kerner taught and cared for children at Woodrow Wilson Day School before joining the City School District for 32 years as a teacher and guidance counselor. She retired at 68 but continued working as needed for two years in the City School District.

"My mother just loved children," her daughter Rachel said. "It never ceased to amaze me, but she couldn't see a kid without hugging him or her."

Mrs. Kerner, who worked at Pine Bluff and William Taft elementary schools, went beyond teaching the basics to help disadvantaged children learn to read and write.

Her daughter said she was a leader in starting the Disadvantaged Child Booster Program, a joint effort by schools and county officials to reach students in low-income and immigrant families. Along with other teachers and staff, she traveled by van to remote communities and taught children English, reading, and writing.

In one case, she helped a young Haitian child develop a love of reading that led to his becoming a New York Times Bestselling Author and Pulitzer Prize winner decades later. He dedicated several of his novels to her.

Beyond providing an education, Mrs. Kerner had a genuine concern for children's well-being. She followed up classroom time in school with notes and phone calls to homes. As a fluent Spanish speaker, she reached out to immigrant families.

"Sometimes kids would say they needed help just so they could go see her; she would give them attention and ask questions about how things were going in school and at home," her daughter said. "Sometimes, they just wanted someone to pay attention to them and listen."

Born in 1939 to a rancher and a dressmaker, the precocious Josephine Wilson spoke Spanish with seasonal laborers as a child. She graduated from St. Mary's Teachers College and later earned a Master's Degree in Education from the University of Florida.

She married Edward Kerner and settled in Jacksonville in 1963. She previously worked for schools in Arizona and Tampa and spent eight years in the private school at Woodrow Wilson.

Mrs. Kerner, who was widowed, enjoyed remodeling her bay-front home. Despite her illness, she pushed workers to complete projects.

"She would drive the contractors crazy," her daughter said. "If she got an idea in her head, she was pretty stubborn about it."

In addition to her daughter Rachel, Mrs. Kerner is survived by a granddaughter, Abigail; a brother, William Wilson; a sister, Agnes Gershaw; and five nieces and nephews.

A memorial service is set for 11 a.m. Thursday at Holy Grace Catholic Church, Olson Lane, Jacksonville. In lieu of flowers, donations may be made to the American Cancer Society Action Network online at https://www.donate.cancer.org.

Acknowledgments

Hello from the Writer's Shed,

Fortunately, I have yet to deal with lingering cancer in my circle of family and friends. My relatives have all gone fairly quickly. And even the few cases of cancer I knew about ended in a few short months, either in death or recovery.

But I have read about things going the other way. And I can imagine the horror of facing death slowly and in agonizing pain. And worse—all alone. As gently as I can put it: we're all dying. But if we're lucky, we're getting the chance—like Jo was trying to do—to enjoy the long twilight.

I hoped with this story to stick to my Stoic outlook and spin things positively. I understand a bleak outlook in any situation, but I want to encourage folks to try and see the beauty and positivity in each moment we have. Because the truth is that all we have are these moments, the Right Nows. The past is already gone an instant after you experience it, and the future is something completely unformed and unknown—and unknowable. So take a moment and pay attention to a sunrise or a grove of trees swaying in the wind or the loved one lying next to you in bed in the morning. Because all of these things will be gone eventually—just like you and I will be. It's important to soak in everything we can for the brief moment of time we're given.

Speaking of time, I know yours is precious; thank you for taking the time to read the words I labored to put to page. If you haven't already, I invite you to leave a review online here. Strong reviews will help get this book into other readers' hands. Writing is like running a marathon—it's a tough struggle. But being read is even harder, with most books slipping into obscurity. So please: tell a friend, post a review on Amazon or mention this book to the person next to you on the train—any help is deeply appreciated.

As usual, I have to thank a couple of people. Writing the first draft is a quiet, private thing. But once I've got it down on paper, I have to let a few sincere eyes look it over before I feel confident to publish it. Charlotte is my forever champion, giving me the golden opportunity to pursue this dogged race called writing. And my Revision Readers (Meta, Kurt, Matt, Brett, and Joshua) help to clear away the mess and get at the marrow of the tale. I thank them from the bottom of my heart and absolve them of any errors herein—they are all mine.

Again, if you'd like to learn about new releases, sign up for my email newsletter.

Thanks for reading!

Teague
Tampa, Florida

About the Author

Teague de La Plaine writes music and stories. He has been variously a Marine Officer, merchant captain, performer, and civil servant.

He lives a charmed life with his charming wife and their little rascals near the sea.

Subscribe to the email newsletter to get updates, deals, giveaways, and FREE stories:

www.teaguedelaplaine.com/subscribe

* 9 7 9 8 8 4 2 2 0 8 4 7 0 *